Look and Find®

DISNEY · PIXAR

LIGHTYEAR

pi kids®

An imprint of Phoenix International Publications, Inc
Chicago • London • New York • Hamburg • Mexico City • Sydney

Buzz Lightyear is on a mission from Star Command! He's testing a new ship, trying to get to hyperspeed so he can get everyone home. He doesn't make it to hyperspeed, but he goes so fast that what feels like a few minutes to Buzz takes four years back at Star Command!

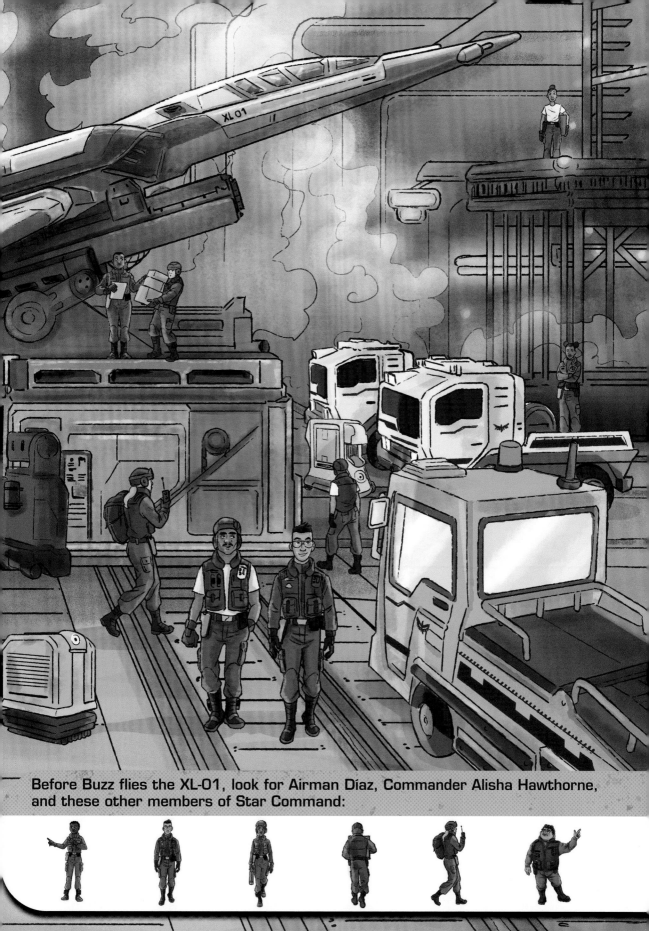

Before Buzz flies the XL-01, look for Airman Díaz, Commander Alisha Hawthorne, and these other members of Star Command:

Buzz and his robot friend Sox finally make it to hyperspeed...but when they land, it's been 22 years. Zap Patroller Izzy tells Buzz that the planet is being threatened by the evil Zurg. Just then, one of Zurg's robotic Zyclopes attacks! As they fight, Buzz realizes Izzy and her friends aren't Space Rangers—they're just trainees.

Find these weapons and ammo the Junior Patrol is still learning to use:

Buzz doesn't want to work with a bunch of trainees. He decides to face Zurg alone. But he needs a ship, so Izzy, Mo, and Darby take him to an abandoned storage depot to get supplies. In the depot, they find the XL-01 and Buzz's old uniform…and a whole nest of giant bugs!

Help the heroes find the things they need—before the bugs wake up:

Meanwhile, Zurg is getting frustrated. He tracks down the XL-15, but by the time he arrives, Buzz is already gone. Then Zurg sends a Zyclops to capture Buzz, but Buzz and his friends destroy it. Zurg decides to deal with Buzz...personally.

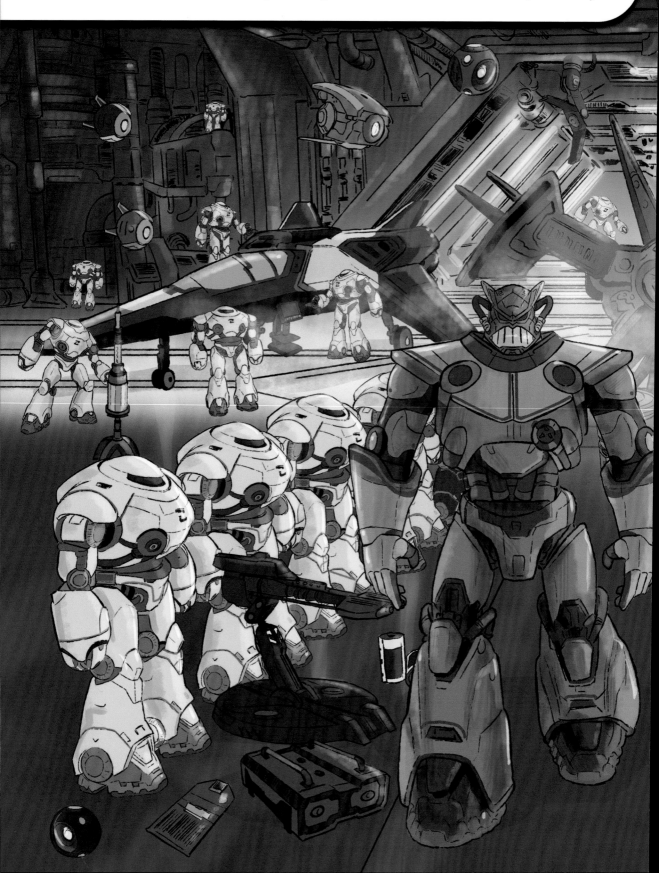

Look around the hangar of Zurg's mothership for the XL-15 and these other devices:

Buzz, Sox, and the Junior Patrol have escaped from Zyclopes and giant bugs, only to be hunted by Zurg himself! Zurg chases them through an abandoned mine, finally cornering Buzz in a canyon. It's a dead end! But Buzz has backup—and they've found some pretty powerful equipment.

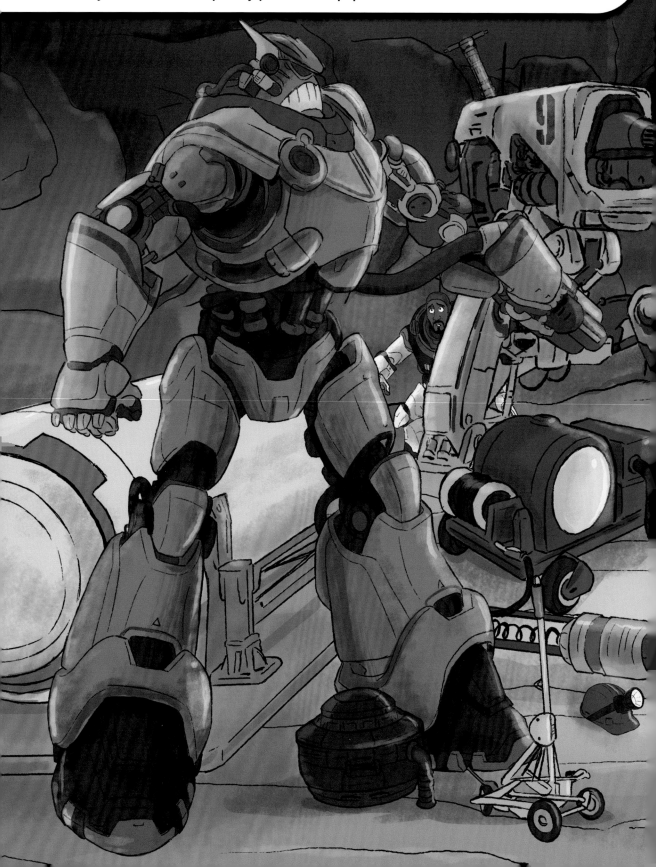

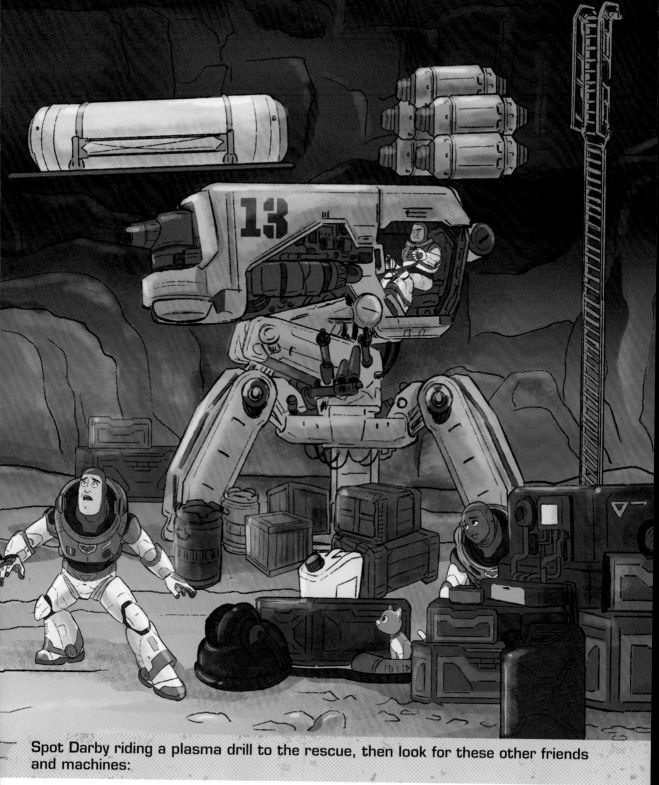

Spot Darby riding a plasma drill to the rescue, then look for these other friends and machines:

Darby blasted Zurg, but the villain is still chasing them—and he's called every single Zyclops to help! If the robots can stick a transport disc onto the Armadillo, they can teleport it up to Zurg's mothership. Buzz hover-drives across a lava field with Zyclopes in pursuit.

Help Mo and Darby hit these Zyclopes before they can catch the fleeing Armadillo:

Zurg doesn't capture the Armadillo, but he does get the fuel crystal—and Buzz! Luckily, Izzy, Sox, Mo, and Darby are coming to help. In the meantime, Buzz is facing Zurg with no backup—and no gravity!

As Buzz struggles to stop Zurg, spot these drifting devices:

Buzz and his friends defeated Zurg...and even managed to land the Armadillo! The heroes have become the perfect team—and when they return to Star Command, they become Space Rangers, too! Together, Buzz, Sox, Izzy, Mo, and Darby are ready to protect the galaxy. To infinity...and beyond!

After the heroes' dangerous landing, look for this safety equipment:

The XL-01 isn't the only vehicle at the spaceport. Fly back to Buzz's first mission and look for these other things on the move:

Zip back to the Zap Patrol outpost and find these gadgets:

Tiptoe back to the storage depot and spot these sleeping bugs:

Head back to the hangar of Zurg's ship and look for these Zyclopes:

Climb back to the canyon and find some more mining materials:

Hover-drive back to the lava field and look for
these transport discs the friends need to avoid:

Float back to the bridge and look for these things:

Fly back to the Armadillo and
find 15 Star Command symbols.